Open a book
and before long you're lost
on seas never crossed
in a dream ship storm-tossed
that will bring you ashore
where no one's yet been . . . .

Turn a page, have a look.
Get lost in a book.

AROUND MY ROOM

Poems *by* William Jay Smith

Illustrations by Erik Blegvad

Farrar, Straus and Giroux ∞ *New York*

To Alexandre Henri from Grandpa in the "Poem Room"—W.J.S

Text copyright © 1990, 1996, 2000 by William Jay Smith
Illustrations copyright © 2000 by Erik Blegvad
All rights reserved
Distributed in Canada by Douglas & McIntyre Ltd.
Color separations by Hong Kong Scanner Arts
Printed and bound in the United States of America by Worzalla
First edition, 2000

"Four Sailors" and "The Chocolate Cake" are freely adapted from Russian poems by Daniil Kharms.

The following poems have appeared in *Laughing Time: Collected Nonsense* by William Jay Smith, published by Farrar, Straus and Giroux in 1990: "Around My Room," "The Mirror," "Having," "The Toaster," "People," "Mrs. Caribou," "Seal," "Polar Bear," "Brooklyn Bridge," "D is for DOG," "The Crossing of Mary of Scotland," "Cow," "M is for MASK," "Raccoon," "Owl," and the limericks "Young Lady Named Rose," "Old Lady Named Crockett," "Explorer Named Hayter," and "Mrs. Piper."

"The Chocolate Cake" appeared in *Food Fight: Poets Join the Fight Against Hunger with Poems to Favorite Foods*, edited and illustrated by Michael J. Rosen, published by Harcourt Brace & Company in 1996.

Contents

Around My Room

I put on a pair of overshoes
And walk around my room,
With my Father's bamboo walking stick,
And my Mother's feather broom.

I walk and walk and walk and walk,
I walk and walk around.
I love my Father's tap-tap-tap,
My Mother's feathery sound.

The Mirror

I look in the Mirror, and what do I see?
A little of you, and a lot of me!

Having

A castle has
    a castle moat,
A river has
    a river boat,
An organ has
    an organ note,
A mountain has
    a mountain goat,
But look at my
    new overcoat!

The Toaster

A silver-scaled Dragon with jaws flaming red
Sits at my elbow and toasts my bread.
I hand him fat slices, and then, one by one,
He hands them back when he sees they are done.

The Cats' Picnic

I saw some Cats beside the road
And I said, "Kitties, come with me.
I'll give you what you love the most,
Bowls of milk, sardines on toast,
All the catnip you desire,
And feather beds by a blazing fire!"

The Cats said, "Thank you, not today,
We're having the picnic of our lives;
We've just unpacked our forks and knives
And tablecloth . . . And here we'll stay."

People

Hour after hour,
In many places,
People sit,
Making faces.

Two Old Friends

Malcolm McTavish came today
    With nothing much upon his mind.
Wild-eyed, wrinkled, old and gray,
Malcolm McTavish came today;
Said: "For a change, try moldy hay
With a little grated lemon rind!"
Malcolm McTavish came today
    With nothing much upon his mind.

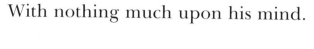

Hilda McDingle came also
    With nothing much upon *her* mind.
Red-eyed, fidgety, and slow,
Hilda McDingle came also;
Said: "Marinate with mistletoe;
It helps the moldy taste, I find."
Hilda McDingle came also
    With nothing much upon *her* mind.

Mrs. Caribou

Old Mrs. Caribou lives by a lake
In the heart of darkest Make-Believe;
She rides through the air on a rickety rake,
And feeds crawfish to a twitchety snake
That sleeps in a basket of intricate weave.
She sits by the fire when the lights are out
And eats toadstools and sauerkraut,
And bowls of thick white milkweed stew.
If you knock at her door, she will rise and shout,
"Away with you, you roustabout!
My cupboard is bare, my fire is out,
And my door is closed to the likes of you!
Go tie yourself to a hickory stake,
Put a stone on your neck, and jump in the lake.
                    AWAY!"

When the fire burns low and the lights are out
And the moon climbs high above the lake,
And the shutters bang, and the ceilings quake,
Mrs. Caribou comes on her rickety rake
And tries to turn you inside out.
But when she does, what you can do
Is snap your fingers and cry, "Shoo!
Away with YOU, Mrs. Caribou!"
Then she will fly back to Make-Believe
With her snake in a basket of intricate weave
And finish her bowl of milkweed stew;
And NEVER come back to bother you.
Shoo, Mrs. Caribou! Shoo, Mrs. Caribou!

Shoo, Mrs. Caribou!

Shoo!

Shoo!

SHOO!

Seal

See how he dives
From the rocks with a zoom!
See how he darts
Through his watery room
Past crabs and eels
And green seaweed,
Past fluffs of sandy
Minnow feed!
See how he swims
With a swerve and a twist,
A flip of the flipper,
A flick of the wrist!
Quicksilver-quick,
Softer than spray,
Down he plunges
And sweeps away;
Before you can think,
Before you can utter
Words like "Dill pickle"
Or "Apple butter,"
Back up he swims
Past Sting Ray and Shark,
Out with a zoom,
A whoop, a bark;
Before you can say
Whatever you wish,
He plops at your side
With a mouthful of fish!

Polar Bear

The Polar Bear never makes his bed;
He sleeps on a cake of ice instead.
He has no blanket, no quilt, no sheet
Except the rain and snow and sleet.
He drifts about on a white ice floe
While cold winds howl and blizzards blow
And the temperature drops to forty below.
The Polar Bear never makes his bed;
The blanket he pulls up over his head
Is lined with soft and feathery snow.
If ever he rose and turned on the light,
He would find a world of bathtub white,
And icebergs floating through the night.

Four Sailors

Yo-ho-ho! . . . And who are we:
Four little Mice who've put to sea
With keen bright eye and waving tail,
A billowing bed sheet for our sail,
And a good stout oar with which to steer.
We flee the creatures that we fear,
Those Whiskered Giants on the shore
Who gaze at us incessantly,
And whom we'd gladly see no more.

Brooklyn Bridge

A Jump-rope Rhyme

Brooklyn Bridge, Brooklyn Bridge,
I walked to the middle, jumped over the edge.
The water was greasy, the water was brown
Like cold chop suey in Chinatown.
And I gobbled it up as I sank down—
  Down—
    Down—
      Down—
        Down—

Brooklyn Bridge, Brooklyn Bridge,
I walked to the middle, looked over the edge.
But I didn't jump off, what I said's not true—
I just made it up so I could scare you;
    Watch me jump!—
      Watch me jump!—
        Watch me jump!—
          BOO!

The Chocolate Cake

Mother decided once to bake
A huge delicious chocolate cake.
How nice of Mother to prepare it;
I asked my friends to come and share it.
They agreed, but they were late,
And so I had to sit and wait.

Their forks were laid out on the table,
And round the cake each empty chair
Sat in gloomy silence there,
Until at last I thought I might
Dare to take a little bite.
And so I did, and then another . . .
And moments later, still another . . .

Then, when my friends knocked at the door,
The cake that was

        was there no more.

Mr. Simpson

A voluminous Person named Simpson
Continually ate curried shrimps on
    Mountains of rice,
    Which was all very nice,
But increased the dimensions of Simpson.

The Kid from Nebraska

Limericks

There once was a kid from Nebraska who
Would never once do what you asked her to.
When they said, "Shut the door,"
She would answer, "What for?"
So they said, "Get back to Nebraska, you . . .
AWFUL KID!"

There exists a Young Girl whose name Tess is,
Whose curls look like capital S's.
She sings soprano
And plays the piano
In stiff white organdy dresses.

There was a Young Lady named Rose
Who was constantly blowing her nose;
Because of this failing
They sent her off whaling
So the whalers could say: "Thar she blows!"

There was a Dumb Dodo named Dorus
Who sang in a high-school chorus.
  When he said, "I'll sing solo,"
  His companions said, "Oh, no,
Please do not, we beg you, you'll bore us."

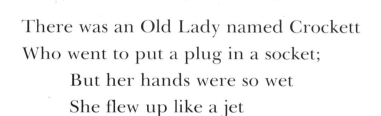

There was an Old Lady named Crockett
Who went to put a plug in a socket;
  But her hands were so wet
  She flew up like a jet
And came roaring back down like a rocket!

An eccentric explorer named Hayter
Sat down on an alligator;
  In the swamp in the fog
  It resembled a log.
Exploration thus ended for Hayter.

D is for DOG

Says the prancing French poodle
As he trots with the band
When it plays "Yankee Doodle":
"Bow-wow! I hate CATS—
The whole kit and caboodle!"

d is for **dog**

The Fat-Cat Circus

There are Cats in the ring
  and Cats on the runways,
And several Cats
  on the flying trapeze.
Clown-kittens out there
  are setting firecrackers;
And Cat Lion-tamers
  have Cats at their knees.
There are Cats on bicycles
  and Cats on white ponies,
Cat-magicians, Cat-jugglers,
  Tomcats, Siamese.
All performers are Cats
  at the Fat-Cat Circus,
And they'll do whatever
  it takes to please.

Timothy Grayling

Handkerchief fluttering,
Timothy Grayling
Climbed up on the railing
To wave to a friend
When the steamship was docking.
The ship gave a lurch;
That settled the matter:
Timothy waved
    and dropped in the water.
Now wasn't that sad?
      Now wasn't that shocking?

The Crossing of Mary of Scotland

Mary, Mary, Queen of Scots,
Dressed in yellow polka dots,
Sailed one rainy winter day,
Sailed from Dover to Calais,
Sailed in tears, heart tied in knots;
Face broke out in scarlet spots
The size of yellow polka dots—
Forgot to take her *booster* shots,
Queen of Scotland, Queen of Scots!

Mrs. Piper

There was an Old Woman named Piper
Who spoke like a windshield wiper.
     She would say: "Dumb Gump!
     Wet Stump! Wet Stump!"
And then like the voice of disaster
Her words would come faster and faster:
     "Dumb Gump! Dumb Gump!
     Wet Stump! Wet Stump!
     Wet Stump! Wet Stump!
Tiddledy-diddledy-diddledy-bump . . .
     Bump . . .
       Bump . . .
         Bump . . .
          BUMP!"
—Which greatly annoyed *Mr*. Piper!

Cow

Cows are not supposed to fly,
  And so, if you should see
    A spotted Cow go flying by
      Above a pawpaw tree
In a porkpie hat with a green umbrella,
  Then run right down the road and tell a
    Lady selling sarsaparilla,
      Lemon soda and vanilla,
So she can come here and tell me!

M is for MASK

It changes a lot
To add a new face
To the face you have got;
Then the person you are
Is the person you're not.

m is for **mask**

Raccoon

One summer night a little Raccoon,
Above his left shoulder, looked at the new moon.
  He made a wish;
  He said: "I wish
  I were a Catfish,
  A Blowfish, a Squid,
  A Katydid,
  A Beetle, a Skink,
  An Ostrich, a pink
  Flamingo, a Gander,
  A Salamander,
  A Hippopotamus,
  A Duck-billed Platypus,
  A Gecko, a Slug,
  A Water Bug,
  A pug-nosed Beaver,
  Anything whatever
Except what I am, a little Raccoon!"

Above his left shoulder, the Evening Star
Listened and heard the little Raccoon
  Who wished on the moon;
  And she said: "Why wish
  You were a Catfish,
  A Blowfish, a Squid,
  A Katydid,
  A Beetle, a Skink,
  An Ostrich, a pink
  Flamingo, a Gander,
  A Salamander,
  A Hippopotamus,
  A Duck-billed Platypus,
  A Gecko, a Slug,
  A Water Bug,
  A pug-nosed Beaver,
  Anything whatever?

Why must you change?" said the Evening Star,
"When you are perfect as you are?
I know a boy who wished on the moon
That *he* might be a little Raccoon!"

Owl

The Owl that lives in the old oak tree
Opens his eyes and cannot see
When it's clear as day to you and me;
But not long after the sun goes down
And the Church Clock strikes in Tarrytown
And Nora puts on her green nightgown,
He opens his big bespectacled eyes
And shuffles out of the hollow tree,
And flies and flies
                and flies and flies,
And flies and flies
                and flies and flies.